This book belongs to:

....

....

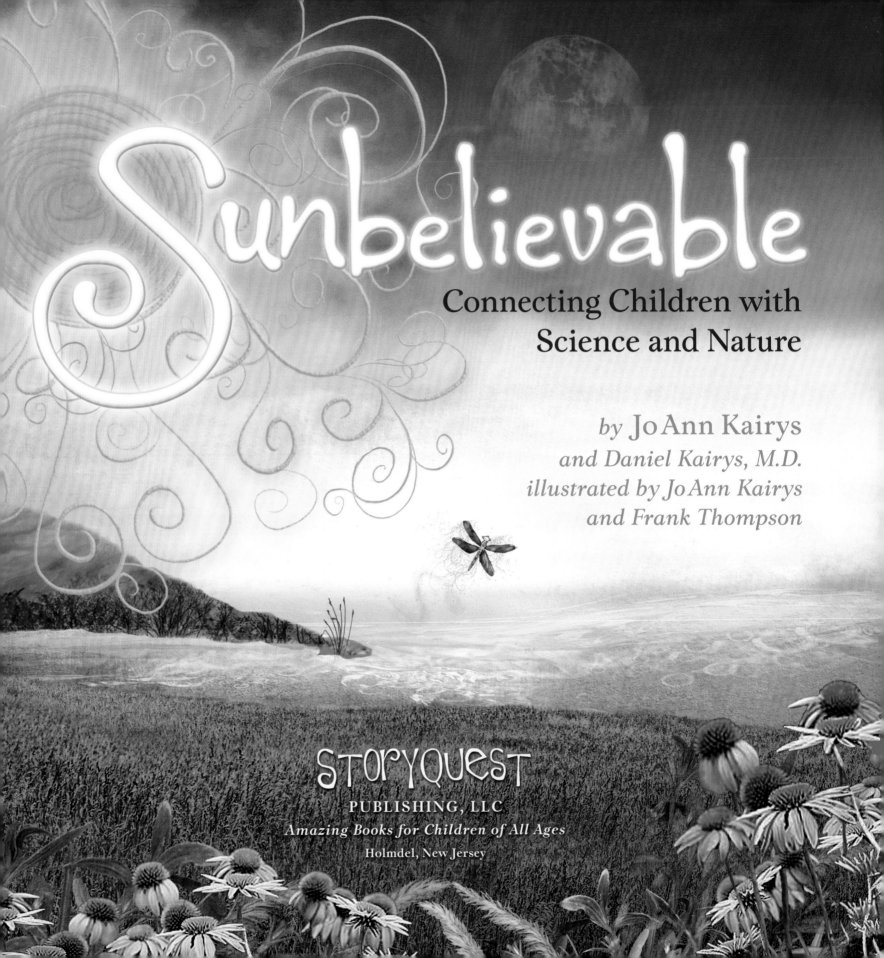

Sunbelievable

Connecting Children with Science and Nature

by Jo Ann Kairys
and Daniel Kairys, M.D.
illustrated by Jo Ann Kairys
and Frank Thompson

STORYQUEST

PUBLISHING, LLC

Amazing Books for Children of All Ages

Holmdel, New Jersey

Published by:

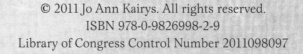

STORYQUEST
PUBLISHING, LLC

Website: StoryQuestPublishing.com
E-mail: info@storyquestpublishing.com
Mailing address: Story Quest Publishing, LLC
1070 Highway 34, #124
Matawan, New Jersey 07747

Book design © 2011 TLC Graphics, www.TLCGraphics.com. Design by Monica Thomas.

Printed in the United States of America.

CPSIA facility code: BP 313943

~ Dedication ~

To our children and their children who, like the sun, illuminate our world.
And to my husband Steve who, every day, makes the world a better place. ~*JK*

To my wife, who incredibly, descended from a meteorite in a hot air balloon
wearing jodhpurs and lugging a caisson of amour, and found me and
said I could have some. ~*DK*

To two grown-ups—one showed me that anything is possible and taught me
how to be a big boy; the other showed me how to love and laugh like a child.
To my wife, Monica, and to my mom, who would be so proud. ~*FT*

YaYa and her little sister Leen
loved to play at the beach.

They filled buckets with slimy crabs
and glittering seashells.

Squishing sand between their toes
felt sensational.

One day, they stayed much too late.
The sun dipped into the ocean and
the sky darkened all around.

"Come on, said YaYa. LET'S GO!"

But Leen did not want to leave.
"It's not so dark—I can still see
my fingers! I want to finish this
tower with you ... making sandcastles
is *my favorite thing* to do!"

"No, Leen, it's time to go!
GET UP!" YaYa insisted.

Leen reluctantly listened to her
older sister and followed her home.

ater, at bedtime, Leen wasn't at all tired. She wouldn't get in bed or even put on pajamas.

"Leen, it's nine o'clock," YaYa said. "Aren't you sleepy?"

"NO!" Leen proclaimed. "I have a great idea! Can we make the biggest sandcastle ever tomorrow?"

Suddenly, before YaYa answered, they heard *knock*...
                    knock...
                              knock.

Daddy opened the door.
"Uh-oh, girls. It's way past bedtime!
We're all waking up early in the
morning for sunrise ... and guess what?
I'll make eggs sunny side up."

Leen frowned. "What's so special
about sunrise and sunny eggs?"

"You'll see in the morning,"
promised Daddy.

YaYa gently combed her sister's
hair and said, "Now, Leen, let's get
to SLEEP!"

"NO! I'm still playing princess!
Five more minutes, YaYa.
Maybe ten? Fifteen? *PLEASE?*
I'm absolutely not tired!"

"But it's time for bed," YaYa patiently
replied. She thought for a moment,
then responded ... "A story always
helps you fall asleep, right Leen?
I just made up a new one to share
with you. Making up stories is
my favorite thing to do!"

"NO! I want to play more,"
Leen demanded. "Well ... what
kind of story?"

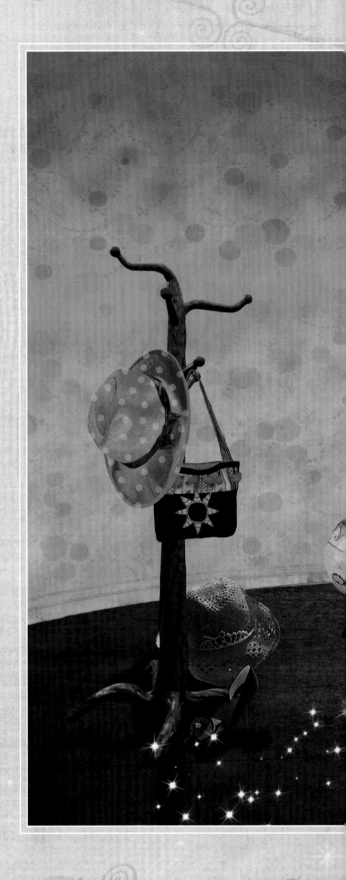

"How about a story of the sun riding a
roller coaster?"

"WHAT? The sun can't ride a roller coaster,
YaYa!"

"YES it does! It races on the coaster
tracks and makes huge shiny sparks."

"HEY! That's silly, YaYa.
Only fireflies sparkle at night."

"Hmmmm. Maybe so, Leen.
But do you know *how* fireflies learn to shine?"

"Professor Sun teaches glowing lessons at Firefly School. That's where fireflies learn to flicker and flash—the brightest flies get gold stars at the end of class."

"WHAT? The sun can't teach fireflies. Tell me a different story, YaYa!"

"Okay, Leen. What about the sun and the garden?"

"*BORING!*"

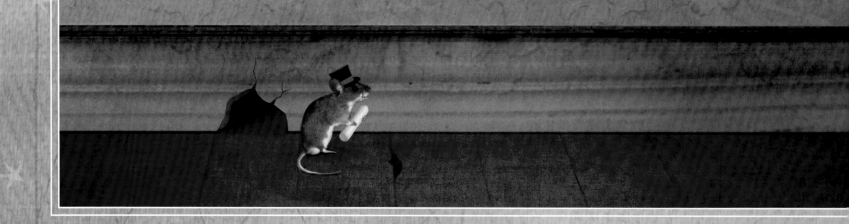

"NO it's not! said YaYa. The sun works hard all day long. It takes zillions of sunbeams to help flowers grow tall. One morning, a sunflower got lost in the weeds and had to ask a dandelion, *Which way is up?*"

"WHAT? Flowers don't talk to each other!" Leen insisted.

"Yes they do! Just like the sun talks to birds!"

"NO it doesn't, YaYa...well, then how?" asked Leen.

"The sun's light wakes all the sleeping birds, and that's how early birds catch the best worms."

"WHAT?" hollered Leen. "Sunlight wakes me up early, but you'll *never* catch *me* eating worms!"

"Oh, really? Then how about this...?"

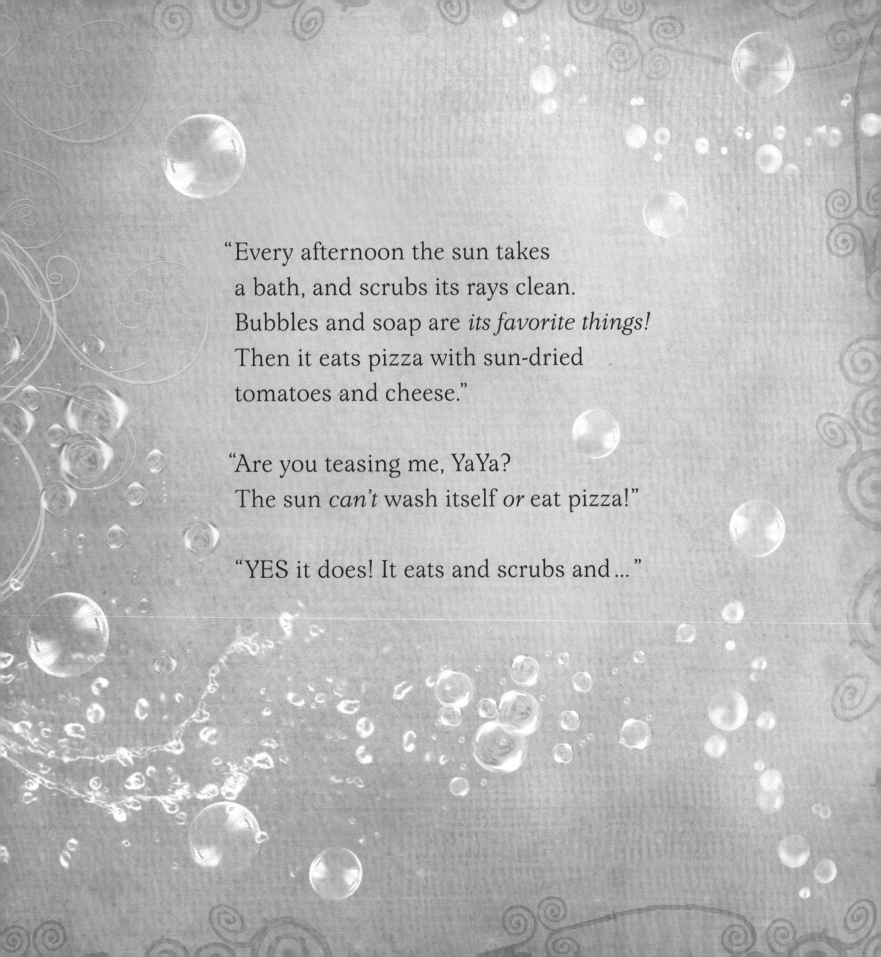

"Every afternoon the sun takes
a bath, and scrubs its rays clean.
Bubbles and soap are *its favorite things!*
Then it eats pizza with sun-dried
tomatoes and cheese."

"Are you teasing me, YaYa?
The sun *can't* wash itself *or* eat pizza!"

"YES it does! It eats and scrubs and ..."

"...YEAH, I get it!" Leen grinned with delight.

She chuckled and added, "And dries out each ray like socks, while resting on its *sun porch*, right? See, YaYa, I can make up stories too!"

Finally, Leen grew tired.
She crawled under her cozy blanket,
but every time she closed her eyes,
they popped wide open again.

I'll pretend to sleep, Leen thought.
If I'm very quiet, YaYa won't hear if
I'm sneaking, away to the beach.
I'll be the first to see sunrise and
early birds down by the shore.

YaYa whispered, "Leen...? Leen...?"
But Leen didn't answer.

YaYa gave Leen a kiss on the cheek and got into bed, but every time she closed her eyes, they popped wide open again.

I'll pretend to sleep, YaYa thought. If I'm very quiet, Leen will think I'm dreaming we soar high in the sky, up to the stars, just like the sun on a coaster ride.

Leen whispered, "YaYa...? YaYa...?" But YaYa didn't answer.

In the morning, Mommy, Daddy, YaYa and Leen saw a spectacular sunrise. "LOOK! LOOK!" YaYa yelled. "The sun is taking off its socks. Its rays must need a good wash!"

"YEAH! Leen shouted. She smiled, and with a twinkle in her eye, she said, "The sun tripped in a puddle of mud and got covered in cobwebs and grimy spiders!"

"RIGHT, we've got it! The sun took a roller coaster ride into the ocean. Now its rays are clean and gleaming!" laughed YaYa.

They gazed at the sky and without another word they knew. Making up stories together was *their most favorite thing* to do.

The Sun in the book Sunbelievable is a magical sun in a fictional story. Our Sun is actually a star—a yellow dwarf star. It is over four and a half billion years old. Our Sun looks small because it is 93 million miles away from Earth.

The Sun gives light and heat to Earth. The temperature of the Sun is nearly ten thousand degrees Fahrenheit. Think about how hot it feels in the summertime when the temperature outside is 80 degrees Fahrenheit! All life on Earth needs the Sun to live and grow, and we need just the right amount.

Each day the Earth rotates once on its axis. Just like a spinning top, the Earth spins around to face the Sun every day. This makes the Sun appear to rise up above the eastern sky in the morning and sink below the western horizon at the end of the day.

The Earth revolves around the Sun once a year in its orbit. As it circles the Sun, it tilts toward and away from the Sun's rays. This is how we experience our changing seasons. It tilts away from the Sun to give us fall and winter, and tilts toward the Sun to warm us in spring and summer.

Because of the Sun's importance to life on Earth, scientists have tried to better understand it through space travel. NASA is planning a daring mission named Solar Probe Plus that will get closer to the Sun than any previous mission. You can learn more about science missions like this and about our solar system by visiting the Web site nasa.gov.

Robert D. Braun, PhD
Chief Technologist
National Aeronautics and Space Administration (NASA)

~ Acknowledgments ~

We are grateful to Junia for unwavering support and mommy love. Zillions of thanks to our true storytellers, YaYa and Leen, for posing on demand and sharing with us their fantastic imaginations.

Thanks to NASA's Robert (Bobby) Braun, an explorer who discovered the mystery of Mars.

We would also like to acknowledge the following individuals for permission to use their graphic artwork and digital design elements.

The "Sunflower Tango" image is © Terri Rosenblum. Terri paints in watercolor and oils and does commissioned paintings and house portraits. terrirosenblumpaintings.com

The digital sun drawing is © Gina Marie Huff. weedsandwildflowersdesign.com

Some of the graphics in the illustrations are © Peggy Derensy of NewLife Dreams. shabbypickledesigns.com

Some of the graphics in the illustrations are © Lorie Davison Poetique Piqutures. Studio Lorie: scrapbookgraphics.com

Thanks to Claudia Marchand for tremendous talent, inspiration and graphic design vision. Thanks to Dave for tremendous encouragement.

The musical accompaniment to the Firefly Lullaby poem heard at www.StoryQuestPublishing.com was composed and performed by Jeffrey DiLucca with vocals by Shayoni Nag.

~ Firefly Lullaby ~

Goodnight, goodnight, goodnight golden sun

Will you come back in the morning?

Goodnight, goodnight, goodnight golden sun

Will you come back in the morning?

Don't fall off the coaster tracks

So you can help all of the fireflies flash.

Linger long in your bubbly bath

And scrub your rays all gleaming.

We need sunbeams to warm up the sky

And help all of the sunflowers grow tall and high.

We need your light so strong and so bright

To help the sleeping birds take flight.

Goodnight, goodnight, goodnight golden sun

I'll see you in the morning!

We invite you listen to the accompanying music
online at StoryQuestPublishing.com.